For Mom,
who inspires me and humors me every day

With special thanks to Art, Doug, Ruby, Katarina,
and the Matchett clan (Mai, Elliot, Peregryn & Juniper)

Henry Holt and Company, LLC. *Publishers since 1866*
175 Fifth Avenue, New York, New York 10010
mackids.com

Library of Congress Cataloging-in-Publication Data
Chung, Arree, author, illustrator.
Ninja! attack of the clan / Arree Chung. — First edition.
pages cm
Summary: Maxwell is a strong, courageous, silent ninja who wants somebody to play with,
but it seems Mama, Papa, and little sister Cassy are all too busy.
ISBN 978-0-8050-9916-4 (hardback)
[1. Ninja—Fiction. 2. Play—Fiction. 3. Family life—Fiction.] I. Title.
PZ7.C4592Niq 2014 [E]—dc23 2015014270

First Edition—2016 / Designed by Arree Chung and Anna Booth
The artist used acrylic paint on Rives BFK paper, found paper,
and Adobe Photoshop to make the illustrations for this book.

Printed in China by Toppan Leefung Printing Ltd., Dongguan City, Guangdong Province

1 3 5 7 9 10 8 6 4 2

NINJA!

ATTACK OF THE CLAN

ARREE CHUNG

Henry Holt and Company
NEW YORK

A ninja must find a **worthy opponent.**

HI-YA!

Mama, want to play with me?
Not now, Maxwell. I'm busy.

Aw...

BOOYAH!
Cassy, want to play with me?
I working.
Oh man, not you too!

Papa!

Yes, Maxwell...

Want to play hide-and-seek with me?

Yes, Maxwell.

OKAY!!!

I'll hide, you seek.

EZ Tax

YOU OWE:

REFUND:

Yes, Maxwell.

A ninja must be **concealed.**

Where should I hide?

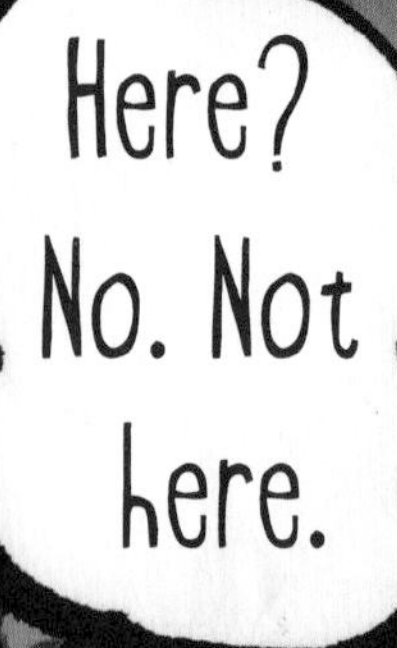

I know . . .
over there!
YIPPEE!
Hee, hee, hee.
Papa will never
find me!

THUMP

THUMP

THUMP

Papa! I'm not in the guest room!

THUMP

Hee
Hee

Hey, you never came looking for me.

BERG
I'm sorry, Maxwell. Did you say something?

Forget it.

A ninja must practice
the art of meditation

and find
inner peace.

Ah!

OUCH!

Maxwell, time for dinner!
All right, I'm coming.

Mama? Papa? Cassy?

Where did everyone go?

Down, boy.

That WAS my miso soup.

WOOF!

WOOF!

SURPRISE

Defend yourself!

ATTACK!

Hi-YA!

Ouch!

You'll pay for that!

I'm gonna get you!

Well, you're no match for me!

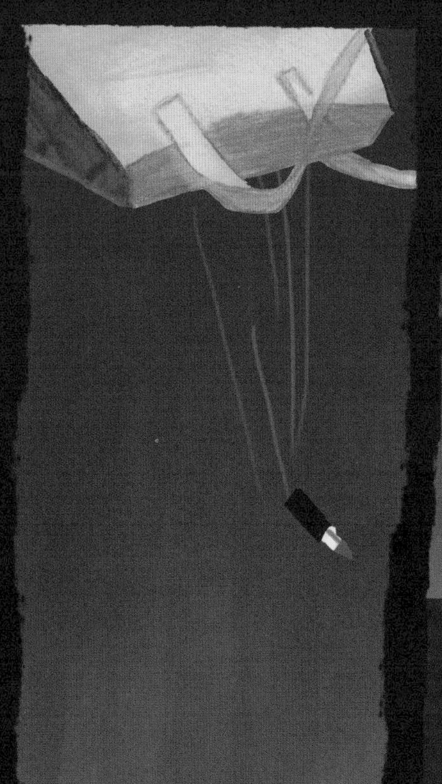

Not the . . .

Yes...the KISS of DEATH!
Two down, one to go.

Come out, come out,
wherever you are!

The little ninja is elusive.

She is small
but powerful.

Ha! Ha!

Ah!

I can't
see!

Ha, ha!
I've got you
now, you sneaky
little ninja!

SLURP!

I've

been

licked.

I love my ninja clan!

wow
I am
a Ninja